MOVING ON

Stories of Longing and Belonging

WILLIAM GEUSS

Published in the United States of America.

ISBN-13:
978-09899147-1-0

Acknowledgements

My thanks to my wife and muse Joan Geuss, to my editor Melissa Schropp, and to the many beta readers who provided valuable feedback and encouragement.

I am also grateful to the members of my writing groups in Evanston, Chicago, and Charlotte for their receptivity and good humor.

This book is for readers who are curious about stories that could happen, if we only let them.

Also by William Geuss

Finding the Way Home

Visit the author's website at
www.williamgeuss.net

The Stories

This collection opens with *The Long Way Home,* which supplies more about the couple featured in *Dumpster Days,* the closing story in *Finding the Way Home.*

The next story, *Water Falls,* shows how rain can upset plans ... or clear the air. And what about rainbows?

In *Help,* a teenager's life gets even more complicated when her parents move to a neighboring town.

In *Burning* unforeseen consequences follow when two brothers make promises to their mother on her death bed ... and then fall in love with the same woman.

A younger sister finds out if a pet can replace her best friend when a growth spurt takes her older sister away from her in *Hello, Pretty Boy.*

In *Georgia, Georgia,* a small-town girl gets transferred to New York City, but it takes a road trip to Georgia to help her find her way in the Big Apple.

Ashes to Asheville follows four generations of a family who look to the past for guidance but no longer see the present clearly nor can imagine a future that differs from the past.

Can a piece of music play a role at threshold moments throughout a man's life? Ralph finds out in *Variations.*

Contents

The Long Way Home

CHICAGO
An Apartment in Lakeview
Josh

Could that be Beth phoning so early? Her mane of hair, rusty-red in the morning sun the day we first met, fills my dreams again. Ever since we parted and I moved into this small apartment, I run into walls in the dark and remember ... our heads bumped when we bent down to untangle the dogs we were walking.

In my confusion, the phone tumbled to the floor and had been ringing far too long for a telemarketer, so I wrenched my legs over the side of the lumpy mattress and squinted at the panel: My buddy Ian was calling from Ireland.

"Josh," he said, "it's been ages since we've talked."

"As near as I can remember, Ian, it was your last night in Chicago." Since he seldom had time for more than a pithy proverb while he kept the bar at the Celtic Isle, anything like a real conversation required that we meet elsewhere—most often at Chicago's Beer Bistro on West Madison.

"So it was," he said, sounding more Irish than when he left for Dublin. "And I got absolutely fluthered."

"That spree did soften the blow when you left, but I miss our talks. Lots has changed. My new apartment is a far cry from the high-rise Beth and I were subletting—as *roommates*," she had insisted. I could barely manage the sixty/forty split on the rent, but thought six months at least gave me a chance to move things beyond roommates to romance.

"I remember," Ian said, "even though I had eight pints that night: You were crushed when the sublet ended, and Burt, the next guy she dated, replaced you."

"It was my own fault, Ian. I had the chance to make a play for her, but I was afraid she'd say 'no'." Changing the subject, I said, "Ian, you must have something important to tell me to call and hang on for that many rings. It's early morning in Chicago … what time is it in Dublin?"

"We're getting ready to open, lad. But, since you always worked crazy hours with your translating, I thought I'd try my luck."

I settled in and pulled enough covers up to ward off the spring chill knowing he would tell me his story once I caught him up on my life. My part didn't take long: I hadn't seen my former flat mate Beth since I moved out of the fancy high rise. Now I made the rent on this dingy studio apartment in Lakeview by translating a four-hundred-page biography of the Swiss chemist who first isolated LSD … and I often wondered if a dose of it might help my outlook on life.

"How is the partnership with your dad going over there, Ian?" I heard typical pub noises of bar stools scraping, glassware clashing, and water running while he thought about it. As a nod both to Chicago (the Windy City) and to legends surrounding St. Patrick (said to have used three-leaf clovers to explain the Holy Trinity), Ian and his father named their Dublin pub the Windy Shamrock. Getting it up and running must have left him precious little free time, so this phone call soothed my feelings of abandonment—first by Beth, and then by Ian.

He told me he and his father had refurbished a tired pub in an under-served area of Dublin with the help of an outfit connected with Guinness which promised 'to revitalize any business with a new exterior façade and interior layout.'

When the medley of background pub noises again filled the pause, I coaxed him, expecting to hear news about Margaret, the woman he lived with during his time in Chicago.

"Do you miss Margaret, Ian?" She liked his Irish accent but tired of how much coaxing it took to get him to talk.

"A woman named Bernadine comes in here two or three nights a week," he offered. "She's got a nice smile and seems to fancy me."

"Then, you're healing faster than I am. I can't get Beth off my mind. Her birthday is coming up. Everyone urged me to gather my courage and tell her how I felt about her. Now, without her in the second bedroom or you at the Celtic Isle to bare my soul to, I'm hurting"—and wondered if that's the lot of writers … and translators?

"To be honest," Ian said, "Bernadine is so different from Margaret that it's bearable. She's Irish and prefers a good listener." Then he changed the subject. "Josh, you ought to come visit me. It could do us both good—like old times. You can bunk with me. Your work is portable. Translation jobs find you no matter where you live. And, don't forget, mate, lots of women come into pubs."

"That is tempting," Ian, "but I'm not sure I have the energy. I'll think about it, though. Thanks for calling and let's keep in touch."

Over the next few weeks, I wrapped up my translation of an optimistic account of the transformative power of LSD, and the idea of visiting Ian began to take root. Why not? A change of scene seems to be working for him. After all, like I heard during my time in Berlin, 'if roast pigeons aren't flying into your mouth while you wait, then it's time to move on.'

The closer Beth's birthday came, the harder it was to get any work done. Drastic action was called for. I handed my neighbor the key to my apartment (his parents were due in Chicago for the summer), and I headed for the airport where I sent Beth this postcard:

"Beth, I've missed being your flat mate! Ian and his dad have a pub in Dublin and invited me to visit: Like John Denver, 'I'm leaving on a jet plane and don't know when I'll be back again.' Have a happy BD; Josh."

DUBLIN, Ireland
June
Josh

I had done it before: Flown to Berlin unannounced, found a translation agency to work for, and stayed a year.

The cheapest flight I found this time put me into Dublin early the next morning with street lights still burning. Traffic into town was light, and the sight of pigeons, perched or strutting about, left me wondering if they knew they have relatives in Chicago?

Forty minutes later, a local bus dropped me and my small duffel and backpack near Ian's pub in a neighborhood of worn, three-story brick buildings, shops at street level and apartments above. In Chicago, this neighborhood would have begged for gentrification but in Dublin, it looked just right. Bleary-eyed, I struck out for the Windy Shamrock on foot.

Cars here drove on the left side, but the screech of brakes at intersections reminded me to Look Right—which was stenciled on the side walk. The lack of clear street signs was less of a hazard, but my airline magazine also cautioned about the paucity of public toilettes. By the time I reached the Windy Shamrock at 10:00 a.m. a trim woman was unlocking the door, and the situation was critical—no stores open, my GPS was speaking Gaelic, and I was desperate for a restroom.

I blurted out my name and predicament and she nodded, pushed the door open and led me to the place I so ardently sought. When I emerged to introduce myself and properly thank her, I learned that she was Fiona, Ian's new stepmother, and recognized me from a selfie that Ian had shot of the blokes at the Beer Bistro during his farewell spree.

While Fiona set up for noon-time trade, I sat at the bar, fighting residual jet-lag, and surveyed the dark wood paneling trimmed with Celtic motifs; a strong cup of her coffee enabled me to chat semi-coherently.

"It's quite homey here," I said, "and feels authentic."

"There was a lot to change when we found it," she said, "but trade has been steady the last six months."

As she busied herself with opening, I learned that, like many other Irish, a wave of prosperity had enticed Fiona to return from abroad, and she met and married Ian's widowed dad.

Hearing this, I dared to hope that the hard times in my love life might one day yield to the same approach. Over the phone, Ian had assured me I would at least have a "good craic" (good conversation, good music and food, and great people) …

"and if that isn't enough," he had added, "the Shamrock's many whiskeys and healthy draft list are sure to fix what ails you."

A flurry of commotion at the doorway drew our attention as a young woman with arms full of packages used her back to push open the door and called, "Dia duit! Fiona (Hello), ... sorry I'm late. By the time I got all these together from the shops, the bus was up the road without me."

"Again, luv? Don't worry, Aileen," Fiona said. "The men folk return from their fishing in two days, and we'll have all hands back on deck."

Aileen squeezed behind the bar and let most of her load tumble to the counter—but for one package, which dropped to the floor. I jumped to scoop it up and reached across to deposit it with the others. "Here you are," I said.

Noticing me for the first time, she thanked me and stepped around the bar and, after a hug for Fiona, hurried over to me.

"Josh," Fiona said, "this is Aileen, Ian's cousin. Aileen, this is Josh, Ian's mate from Chicago."

"Ian and I met in Chicago about a year ago," I explained. "When he called me recently, he could tell I needed a change and insisted I come visit."

"Well, at this point, you do look the worse for wear," Aileen said. "I hope you'll be staying long enough to feel at home ... and won't lose your American accent," she added with a mischievous smile.

"Thank you," I said, and shook the hand she held out while regular patrons of the Shamrock began to arrive.

As the morning wore on, Aileen and Fiona heartily welcomed everyone who entered and introduced me as Ian's chara (pal) from Chicago. Many of those who joined us told of kin who left for America—and of some who had returned.

Despite a second cup of Fiona's coffee, I must have begun

to fade because Aileen noticed my eyelids drooping and asked "Where will you be staying, Josh?"

"Ian spoke of putting me up," I said, stifling a yawn, "but I didn't warn him when I was coming."

"Here's what we'll do then," Fiona said. "Aileen will serve here with me tonight, but I can manage for now while she takes you around to Ian's place and gets you settled in. Come back over later for supper."

Aileen beckoned and smiled broadly, "Come along Josh. We can walk. It's not far," she said and led the way out to the street.

Hurrying to keep up on leaden legs, I noticed how trim hers looked and how sprightly she moved. "Do you live near the pub," I asked?

"About a twenty-minute bus ride," she said. "Is this your first visit to Ireland, Josh?"

"My second; I was in Berlin for a year and then stopped through on my way to Chicago. I needed to get my feet on the ground," I replied, leaving it at that rather than mentioning the four objectives taped above my desk in Chicago: '1. Work enough to pay the rent; 2. Find friends; 3. Get laid; and 4. Find love.'

"You'll like it here," she assured and took us on a route that taxed my ability to memorize landmarks for the trip back to the Shamrock. This went well enough until my toe caught on a cobblestone, and I would have fallen had Aileen not bent to grab one handle of the duffle and right me. "No need to play the strong man, Josh," she said as we carried on side by side, "Irish gals appreciate a chance to show their stuff."

To tell the truth, it was rather nice to receive so much attention. So far, I was truly content to be back in Ireland … without further thoughts of Beth.

Ian's Apartment

By the time we reached Ian's entryway and she handed me the key he had left with her, I learned that Aileen lived with her mother; her two younger brothers had left for Canada four years earlier, but she made no mention of her father.

I looked around the tidy apartment. "It doesn't look like Ian spends much time here."

"No, he doesn't," she said, picking up a photo of Ian serving an attractive, dark-haired woman at the Shamrock who reminded me of Ian's Margaret in Chicago. Tapping the photo, she added, "He's quite happy to be back in Ireland—especially since he met Bernadine."

Then I asked, "Aileen, could you imagine living abroad like your brothers do?"

"That I can, but I'll be with my mum—or close by as long as I have her. Her voice tightened, then broke as she said … "My dad died last year."

I could think of nothing to say and my hand went up to squeeze her arm which she took as an invitation to embrace. When I released her after a few moments, I hoped she had found this as comforting as I.

With shining eyes, she said, "You're a good listener, Josh. I hope you'll tell me your story, once you've rested up." Then she turned and set out for the Windy Shamrock.

CHICAGO
Precinct Towers Highrise Apartments
Beth

"Lighten up, Burt! That was the first time I heard from Josh after he moved out six months ago. What are you doing going through my drawers, anyway?" I said as he waved Josh's farewell postcard in my face. "Josh was a roommate. We parted friends, we shared the rent ... nothing else."

This was mostly true—although there were moments when Josh and I seemed on the threshold of something more. But now was not the time to mention it, as Burt stormed out the door.

I couldn't help wondering if I rushed things when Burt moved in, but I was sure it would work out better than previous times when guys disappointed me.

Work and adjusting to Burt had sapped so much energy that I neglected regular chats with Rhonda, my roommate before I moved downtown to share a place with Josh. I always felt better after I bared my soul to her and managed to reach her at lunch today.

After catching up on her and her guy, Henry, and laying out my confusion, she said, "All I know is the experience you had with that guy in college messed you up—and you kept your draw bridge up until you met Josh."

"That's true. When we talked about moving in here together and Josh told me he was hoping for more than 'roommates', but I made it clear where I drew my line."

"Do you ever have second thoughts about the roommate thing?" Rhonda asked. "I know I still wonder whether I did the right thing inviting Henry to move in with me."

"If you hadn't done that, I wouldn't have moved out to make room for him. Sharing the Precinct Towers sublet with Josh downtown solved my problem: I couldn't stand that commute anymore."

"No, I mean about choosing Burt over Josh," she said.

Noticing the time, I said, "I admit that has been keeping me awake. Sorry, Rhonda, I've got to go now. I'm meeting Burt at the Berghoff for some German beer at 6 p.m.—and I still have a ton to do."

"OK. About the German beer—just remember our heritage; we're Wisconsin girls and know a thing or two about beer."

"Right. Bye."

To judge from the taxi horns as I walked the few blocks from my office at the Chicago Tourist Bureau to the Berghoff Restaurant, traffic was more impatient than usual, and I was very glad not to have a forty-minute commute home. Living downtown had its advantages, but the gusting wind left me uncertain whether I was headed for a storm or for genuine relief from the latest hot spell with Burt.

He seemed more distracted the past few days. Hank, his best buddy from their fraternity days at Northwestern was getting married in three weeks, and Burt was planning the bachelor party. For one thing, Hank was a guy I didn't especially like; for another, it always took Burt a couple of days to straighten up after they went out.

Tonight, I managed to relax—the considerate, funny Burt, who had been hired away from the Milwaukee Tourist Bureau showed up for German food and beer.

A few days later, Stan, our team leader, called a meeting at the last minute which did not involve Burt. Since I worried it might go over like a lead balloon dropped from our 26th-floor apartment, I left Burt a message: "Hey, Burt, Stan called another last-minute meeting. I'll be late tonight. Sorry. Go ahead and eat something, and I'll be there as soon as I can. Bye."

The Windy Shamrock Pub
Three Weeks Later

Josh

After two months, Dublin was wearing quite well. Staying at Ian's apartment worked out because it gave him an excuse to stay more often at Bernadine's, and it came as no surprise when he told me they were planning to get engaged.

"Why that is fabulous news, Ian. She suits you well."

"A serious occasion calls for some serious drink, mate," he said. "How does Sunday here after closing please you?"

"I'll count on it."

The last guests were being sent off with hearty goodbyes as I arrived at the Shamrock on Sunday and hailed Ian.

When he had drawn us each a pint of Guinness, we repaired to the snug while the barman on duty finished closing up. Ian said, "After our time in Chicago, it's almost treasonable to be celebrating here in Dublin rather than at the Beer Bistro in Chicago."

"It is hard not to be a little homesick," I said. "After all, the Bistro resembles an Irish pub. They brought their snug—complete with etched, colored glass and antique fireplace—from Dublin."

By the time we had moved through the salient differences between the two settings—such as how the relative advisability of ordering Irish car bombs in a bar improved the further away one was from where the troubles had played out—it seemed natural to pass on to yearnings and doubts regarding our own lives, and I learned enough more about Bernadine, Ian's intended, to look forward to getting better acquainted with her.

For his part, Ian got to hear my semi-coherent pipe dream of a future scenario that shifted from missing the life I had known in Chicago to how I would miss life as I was getting to know it here in Dublin—including Aileen who visited me when Ian's apartment was available and in the dreams that previously had only featured Beth's mane of rusty-red hair.

"Well, this may not come as a surprise, Josh, but Aileen let on to Bernadine that she hopes you will be staying."

CHICAGO
Precinct Towers Highrise Apartments

Beth

Friday, the night of Burt's bachelor party for Hank arrived. I was still planning to head up to Milwaukee after work and visit women I knew from meetings in Chicago—but I couldn't help wonder what Burt was up to. He had been a mess while he was arranging the whole thing, and I hadn't been particularly sympathetic. To smooth things over, I decided to call him at the party.

When he picked up, all I could make out was catcalls and whistles and the slurred words: "Call me tomorrow," before the line went dead.

Great, I thought and left a text message:

> *Hey Burt, have fun, but you don't need to keep up with Hank at the party tonight. I care about you, even if I think Hank is a ****. See you Sunday night. Beth*

He immediately texted back:

> *"Well duh. That's the whole idea here. If you think you can torpedo my friendship with Hank, my best buddy since freshman year at NU, forget it. While we're at it, what gives with all your extra meetings since Stan arrived?"*

I remembered Rhonda saying her Henry gets like that too, so I decided to ignore it—guys can be such jerks.

Sunday night around 10:30, I got home from Milwaukee and all was quiet. No note. No messages. Now it was my turn to wonder what was up. I tried his number and got: 'The party you are calling is not available; please try again later.'

I tried to think of an explanation I would accept. Is he OK, I wondered? Then that familiar feeling from high school and college came back: Has someone walked out on me again, or am I just being weird? What's wrong with him having a little fun? Dammit! I wasn't going to let myself be treated like that.

Burt turned up well after midnight. When I asked him who he was with, I got, 'I'm not up for an inquisition—just out celebrating some more,' and felt the familiar fear beat against my chest.

By morning, I had decided I'm overreacting, but when I made the bed and gave the covers on my side a flip, something fell to the floor. I bent down and found a strange earring. Drastic scenes played in my head, as I backed away from the bed, shaking my head.

I left before he woke the next morning and walked to the office to calm down. I wanted to give Burt a chance to explain, so I left a note on the breakfast table with the earring attached that said, "What's this earring doing in our bed?"

When I got home that night, he was already there, as though nothing happened. "So, what's with the earring," I asked.

"Oh, that." he said. "My cousin Trina and her girlfriend stopped through Chicago on their way to Tokyo. I let them sleep in our bed because they had an early flight. By the time I woke up, they had grabbed a cab to O'Hare."

"It's funny you never mentioned her before."

"Just cut the inquisition. If you get over it, we can still go out for dinner. Where would you like to go?"

For several days, things were strained between us, but one question was making me crazy: *How Burt turned out to be so different from what I had expected? Was it a big mistake to let Josh get away?* Then, work stress trumped personal stress and things evened out without any ultimatums.

A week later, Burt shook me and I heard him grumble, "Beth? Yeah, she's here. Just a minute."

He rolled towards me in bed and said, "Beth, somebody wants to talk to your old roommate." He handed me the phone but didn't release it. "This has gotta stop, Beth, it's the middle of the night."

"Give it here, Burt," I said and had to tug the phone away from him. It was Josh's sister.

"Hi. Amy? No, I don't have a number for Josh. ... Gosh, I'm sorry to hear about Travis. Yeah, I can understand you wanting to phone him instead of sending an e-mail. Josh didn't go on about him, but I know he worried about his brother. You're coming up to Chicago? Look, you'd be welcome to stay with us."

"Ouch," I said as Burt punched me in the side. "No, I'm ok, ... my boyfriend will have to understand. We aren't far from that hospital. Just let me know when you get to town. Josh sent me a postcard when he left for Ireland, but there was no contact information. I'll try and get a phone number and ask him to call you. You've already got your hands full."

"What's the big idea, Beth?" Burt groused as I hung up.

I sat up and said, "Look, there's nothing to worry about. That was, Josh's sister, Amy, in Ohio. I put up with you through the whole party-for-my-best-buddy-thing—so now you can just accept that I am doing the right thing for a friend of mine."

I took it as positive that Burt listened without comment, so I continued. "She hadn't heard from Josh in months and just learned that their brother Travis is in intensive care here in Chicago. She doesn't have a phone number for Josh anywhere and wondered if he left one with me. She wants to tell him, rather than drop an e-mail on him."

I knew Josh worried about Travis from what he shared. They had an alcoholic father who took his disappointments in life out on Travis and a mother who felt powerless to change any of it. The fact that Josh and I had shared much more with each other than I had with Burt made me uneasy.

I thought I might be in for a rough time at breakfast, but Burt slept in and called me later to say he wouldn't be home for dinner—something about Hank.

It took me an hour cross-searching on the Internet to track down newer pubs in Dublin with names that sounded like possibilities but some would not open for several hours.

At the third one I tried, The Windy Shamrock, a woman named Aileen answered and knew right away who Josh was.

I was about to leave work when Amy called again. "Hi Beth, it's Amy. I'm in Chicago. Travis is stable and may get moved from ICU in a few days. But I haven't heard from Josh."

"I left a message two days ago with a woman in Dublin named Aileen who helps out there. She said Josh wasn't there but promised to pass it along."

"I don't know what to do, Beth."

"Listen, Amy, you've got your hands full with Travis and the hospital. I'll call the Shamrock in Dublin again and ask them to tell Josh. And, Amy … I do hope your brother makes it."

DUBLIN
The Windy Shamrock
Josh

I was just arriving at the Windy Shamrock and ran into Aileen as she came out.

"Hello, Josh. You look as tired as when you first got off the plane. "Do you remember?" Aileen asked and put her hand on my arm.

"I do. I was up late last night again meeting a deadline and thought I would stop in for a pint and some lunch at the Shamrock before a good nap."

"A good laugh and a long sleep are the two best cures for everything," she said, "and, forgive me if another thing also comes to mind."

I blushed. "That crosses my mind, too," I said and changed the subject. "How has your mom been lately?"

"She's slipping—she can't seem to remember enough to finish what she sets out to do."

"That sounds right enough for her age."

"But what worries me more is her bad cough. She can't shake it, and the doctor says pneumonia could be the end of her. I'm taking her in today."

"That is serious."

"My turn to change the subject: You know, Josh, I've noticed more women coming into the Shamrock since you've arrived, and I've been talking with my gal friends. I'm not the only one who likes to hear your accent."

"They'll get used to it soon enough, Aileen, but after talking with Ian the other night, I think there are much worse things than a longer stay in Dublin."

"You won't be hearing any objections from me. Well, look at you—I didn't know you were the blushing type, Josh. Now

I'd best be getting along home since I can't keep the doctor waiting."

Josh and Ian

By the time I saw Ian arrive an hour later, lunch, a pint, and thoughts about Aileen had smoothed my outlook on things considerably.

"Hello, Ian, if you don't mind me saying, you look troubled."

"Let's go over to the snug in the corner, Josh. It's more private and there is something you need to know about."

When we were seated in a corner booth, I said: "OK. Ian, tell me."

"I just got a phone call from Beth, your old flat mate. She's trying to get a message to you to call your sister, Amy."

"Really? Did she say what it's about?"

"Only that your brother is in the hospital and your sister is staying with Beth."

"My God! Thanks, Ian. I was searching for Travis the whole time I was in Chicago."

"If you don't mind me asking, why is that?"

"I need to tell him ... 'I'm sorry' ... sorry for letting him be the one to take all the abuse from our dad; I let Travis down. And it cost him dearly."

I explained that Travis gave up on college and spent years drifting before moving to Chicago; now, as a homeless vagrant, he spends his days dumpster diving. I always felt guilty about escaping the brunt of our father's outbursts, and the hope of finding my brother was what had drawn me to Chicago after Berlin.

Ian looked down. "There's more, mate. Beth said your sister called here two days ago and spoke with Aileen—who promised to pass a message along to you."

"I saw Aileen this morning, Ian, and she didn't say a word about that."

"She'll be the one who knows why—but taste your words before you spit them out, mate; many is the time a man's mouth broke his nose."

Although I had been in Dublin three months already, I was still no better at teasing out the meaning of Irish proverbs than when Ian dished them out in Chicago.

"Beth left these for you," he said and handed me phone numbers for both Beth and Amy.

As he left, I thanked him and got on the phone, grateful for the privacy the snug provided. When I got Amy at the hospital, she told me that Travis had relapsed and was back in ICU. He was having fluid drained from his lungs and took a turn for the worse. I knew I had to get to Chicago as soon as possible.

Getting to the bottom of things with Aileen would have to wait.

CHICAGO

Beth

I had been so preoccupied with how things stood with Burt that I had also neglected my heart-to-hearts with Corinne. To remedy that she suggested we meet in Millennium Park where we found a bench near beds of lilies and a fountain. I relaxed while she filled me in on her past few weeks.

"So tell me girl, what's on your heart today?"

I had always been able to depend on Corinne for careful listening, and this time was no exception. "Burt is barely handling Amy staying with us while she visits Travis in the hospital. I can't imagine how weird he might get if Josh were to stay here too. I told him, just imagine if your buddy Hank were in a fix like this, wouldn't you want to help him out? It should be no big deal."

"Wow, so it's Burt vs Josh in the center court."

"Yeah. I don't know how much more of it I can take. After Josh roomed with me for six months and we found a good fit together … I thought he would come forward with feelings for me, but he didn't; instead, he mentioned money worries and didn't say anything about wanting to stay. I had my hopes up and was desperate to protect myself from getting hurt, so I showed him the door when our lease was up; that's when Burt made his move."

"Remember, Beth, it's never too late to have a talk with Josh. He'll be here in Chicago. Why don't you see if you can straighten some of this out?"

"I told Amy to tell him they both can stay with us while they're here."

"Does Burt know yet?"

"I wanted to wait until I know when Josh is arriving … he might not even come."

DUBLIN
The Windy Shamrock Pub
Aileen and Fiona

Several days later, as Aileen was helping close after a raucous evening, Fiona asked, "Aileen, you act like the lark is gone from your sky. What do you hear from Chicago?"

"Josh looked so sad when he first arrived in Dublin. I had hopes of giving him what he's lacking … but he always seems distracted when we're together," she said and began gathering up the small oil lamps from the tables for refilling. "I doubt that my mum will be around much longer," she continued, "and there isn't anyone around I could see for me to care about." A lamp slipped from her hand and oil spread in a small puddle on the table; she burst into tears.

Fiona took her in her arms and held her until she regained her composure. She said, "There was a time when a girl would not tell her fella everything or would say anything to keep him from leaving. I even know one who told her fella she thought she was pregnant to keep him home."

"To tell the truth, I've thought about that too," Aileen said, as she continued blotting up the oil.

"I can only tell you, it was a mistake for you not to tell Josh about the phone call. Ian told me that if his brother dies and he doesn't get there in time to say goodbye, Josh won't find it easy to forgive."

"I was just so afraid he would leave and not come back," she said and burst into tears again.

CHICAGO

Amy and Josh

"Hi, Amy, it's Josh. I'm at the airport," he said, speaking to be heard over an announced change of arrival gate.

"Thank God, Josh. This has been hard."

"At least we have Travis back after the years of uncertainty."

"I'm glad you got here in time, but it's touch and go. He's back in ICU and doesn't know what's going on."

"I want to see him as soon as possible. I appreciate all you have done. What do you suggest?"

"You can take the 'L' Train to the medical center from the airport; call me when you get here, and I'll meet you in the ICU waiting area. I've been staying at Beth's and she insists that you stay there too."

"I'm not so sure that's a good idea."

"Why?"

"It's all tied up with the way things ended between Beth and me. I hid behind my money worries and hesitated too long. And she had someone waiting in the wings. I can't stop thinking about what might have been. I feel stupid; it was my own fault."

"Don't worry. We can talk more later, Josh."

"OK. I'll come as fast as I can."

Later that day

Beth

Burt was rushing out the door and brushed past me as I got home from work.

"Where's the fire?" I asked.

"Hank invited the guys out tonight who threw the bachelor party. We're going to Rush Street. Don't worry," he sniggered over his shoulder and headed for the elevator, "it's a stag party, and I'll be late."

"By the way, Josh flew in this afternoon," I called after him, "and he and Amy will be staying here. Travis isn't expected to live much longer."

He hit the brakes and took a step back towards me. "So, you're asking me to make room for your old boyfriend?"

"We've already discussed that. He never was a boyfriend."

"Look," he snapped, "if you insist on having him here, count me out. I've had enough."

"Well, so have I, Burt. And I'm through waiting for you to grow up."

He shook his head and started towards the elevator again. "I'm going out with guys who see things my way. I'll be back tomorrow to get my things."

"Good. And you can take that earring back to its owner—if you can even remember her name!"

William Geuss

CHICAGO
Three days after Travis died
Josh and Beth

After another hectic day spent with arrangements for Travis' cremation, Amy retired early, leaving me seated on the couch with Beth to digest how this chapter in our lives had closed: Travis had returned briefly, only to leave us again, and Burt had failed to prove a lasting companion for Beth.

Her mood was subdued, and I saw traces of relief and disappointment in her face as the buildings visible from what had been *our* apartment for six months now darkened into night. Memories of the times we watched them take their places in the nighttime cityscape resurfaced—but I didn't know where to start as we sat in silence.

Perhaps it was simpler to look ahead than to go back because Beth asked, "What are your plans now, Josh?"

"Travis chose to live in Chicago, but we want him near Amy, in our mom's plot in Ohio. Amy is leaving tomorrow. I appreciate you letting us stay with you, Beth."

"And what will you do now?"

It felt weird to be back, but seeing Beth again helped me sort through feelings about our time together. "It was grand to see Ian in Dublin ... I was starting to make a place for myself there. But when you and I moved in together and you drew the line at 'roommates, not romance,' I didn't have the courage or the sense to challenge it ... now, I can see I should have listened to the advice everyone was giving me."

"What was that?"

"It was to roll the dice and just kiss you," I said, and put my arms around her, startling her. Then I kissed her, lingering long enough to gauge any objections.

She leaned into my embrace and said, "When our lease was

over the pile of presents to reach him, trying not to step directly on any. When he saw what Roger was up to, he clapped his hands and said, "Get out of there boy."

Roger flew around wildly for a minute and we all cheered when he landed on Momma's shoulder and said something that sounded like "Pretty Boy."

We laughed so loudly he flew away and bounced off a wall before heading back to land on his cage. After wobbling a bit, he got right on Judy's finger without biting and let her guide him back into the cage.

"Roger, it's time for bed now," she told him and carried the cage back into our room as we all wished, "Merry Christmas, Roger."

The next morning, I awoke to Judy's scream. Roger lay on the floor of the cage with his feet in the air.

Daddy came in and when he saw Roger on the floor of the cage, he said, "Well Honey, I guess Roger got too much Christmas"—but that didn't help at all.

Even though it was Christmas Day, Nelson still managed to telephone Judy, and I overheard her tell him the bad news.

When Mother suggested to Judy that she might like to get another bird, she said, "No, Mother. I don't think I'll have enough time for another bird. And I have been wondering, do you think I could have my own room now? Nelson has a younger brother and they each got their own rooms this year."

"Well, we will have to talk to your father, but I don't see why not."

So, Judy and I parted ways that year. And things never were the same. Maybe the fact that I got a pet rat and named him "Nelson" had something to do with it.

Georgia, Georgia

One Saturday in late September in New York City, Trish Gentry was scrubbing the toilet in the low rent apartment she shared with another flight attendant in Murray Hill, close to the Midtown Tunnel, when her smart phone pinged. Grateful for the distraction, she gave the bowl a last swirl and wiped the perspiration from her forehead. At least her roommate Faye got this duty next weekend.

Stripping off her vinyl gloves, she started for the kitchenette to check her phone on the counter when it pinged again, *OK!*– two new texts from Larry, the guy she had been seeing the last three months. She swiped and tapped.

The first, from three minutes earlier, read: "*Leave tomorrow for N. GA. Come watch me at work! L.*" The next: "*What's keeping u?*"

His assumption she could drop everything for him nettled her but the attention was flattering. And he was ambitious: 'You'll see, Trish. I'll make it into *The New Yorker*' but his certainty made her uneasy. Was that what it took to succeed in New York?

Was she still just a shy girl from the plains of Kansas? Maybe it was her figure and her shiny, chestnut hair that landed her the job—some of the older airline crew hinted as much. And in Larry's case, was she just an ornament for a guy on the make? His attention had already led her to behave in ways her grandmother would disapprove of—but her grandmother had not grown up in the Big Apple. As it was, she didn't fly again for another four days, so she texted him back: "I'll come."

She had met Larry at a party soon after *GO*, the regional airlines she crewed short-haul flights for, transferred her to NY along with Faye, someone she knew from the Pittsburgh hub. Fortunately, a seasoned colleague had told them, "First of all, canvass buildings in the Murray Hill neighborhood. Check with the supers in any with more than thirty units—those are less likely to lose their rent control status"—and in two days, they found something affordable.

A month later, when both she and Faye were in town and she felt settled enough to join Faye in exploring New York nightlife, they heard about a party in a Battery Park high rise. As they exited the elevator on the fifteenth floor, loud voices spilled out of an apartment at the end of the hall.

Once inside, Faye quickly disappeared in the mix of airline people and others Trish didn't recognize. Instinctively, she turned as if to head for the door but found herself looking into the hazel eyes and sharp features of a trim, wiry man slightly taller than she, who stood quite close. He simply said: "I'll bet you're new to the Capitol of the World," and she couldn't think of a reply.

Although Larry's brashness sometimes made her uneasy, going places with him made it unnecessary for her to screw up the courage to meet new people, and she considered herself lucky.

That was three months ago and, by now, she was not so sure about the luck part. But, when his two texts came in and she didn't have other plans, she decided to go along to Georgia.

The next day, her standby privilege got her on an early flight to Atlanta International, and by nine o'clock, they had met up and headed north in Larry's rental car, a blue compact with orange NY plates that stood out from most other vehicles.

When he pulled over a few blocks from the airport, she asked, "Larry, why are we stopping? You haven't really told me what you're going to work on down here." He had only hinted that it was for a piece he had been thinking about writing for some time.

"It's an election year, Trish, and everyone (by this, he meant everyone in NY) will read a piece about what a black candidate for president is up against in red states. Georgia has been red the last three elections. *The New Yorker* will want this piece."

She watched as he got out and took something from his briefcase, moved around to the rear of the car, and bent down. Several minutes later he dropped some strips of paper on the ground and stepped back in, looking pleased.

"What was that all about?" she asked.

"Remember high school chemistry and litmus paper? You know the stuff that ended up blue, pink, or red?"

"Kind of."

"Well our NY car now has election bumper stickers—the equivalent of litmus paper. We're going to find out what they provoke down here."

Something in his voice led Trish to believe he was sure of the outcome, and she wondered about the ethics of this approach. She could understand his ambition to break into big-time journalism, but was there more to this than that? Once, he had mentioned that his mother was from Atlanta and had left his domineering father when Larry was barely ten. Another time, he let slip that his father blamed his mother when he put Larry in a boarding school. Was he just trying to even some kind of score?

As if in answer, he sped up and overtook a car that had passed him on the right; then he swerved over in front of it and slowed to the speed limit, provoking a horn salvo.

"Take that, Cracker!" he replied.

"Larry, is this part of your experiment or do you always drive like this? Maybe it's not your bumper stickers."

"Trish, don't be a spoil sport."

The seven miles from the airport north into Atlanta were much the same and left her on edge—but she had to admit that the blue car with NY plates was not the only one that appeared to be on an adversarial course.

When they left the city and rejoined the highway, he said, "So far, my litmus test isn't conclusive. But I'm having a great time. And another thing: I want to check out the ridiculous claim that wine guy, Charlie Hanson, made in *The New Yorker* that 'Georgia wines rival upstate New York's.' Now that *would* be newsworthy."

Relieved at this concession and the added focus on something more agreeable, Trish nodded off to the hum of tires and slept until he abruptly slowed to leave the interstate and begin climbing north toward the Blue Ridge Mountains. Through a yawn, she said, "If anybody honked at your bumper stickers, I didn't hear it."

"It's hard to tell so far. There have been lots of out-of-state plates. We'll have to give the towns and hills a try."

Just after five p.m., Larry pulled into a café on the edge of a small town and squeezed between two large pickups with red clay covering their wheels and rifle racks visible in their rear windows. Other trucks carried tool chests and gear related to construction work. Some sported bumper stickers; all had Georgia plates.

They stepped out and Trish stretched. "Can you smell it, Larry? This isn't city air. It's kind of piney and ... like warm rock."

Instead of replying, he said, "Get a load of this, Trish," and read: *If You Like Osama, Vote Obama!* And *GUN CONTROL ... means using both hands*, and exclaimed, "now, this is more like it."

Before he could read any more, she tugged on his coat and said, "Come on, Larry, I'm hungry."

They entered the café and stood for a moment as the smell of fried food washed over them and all eyes shifted to the trim newcomers.

Larry glanced around and saw a mix of curiosity and suspicion amid elbow poking. "Trish, I have a hunch this will be easy," he whispered, but his smile looked forced.

"That's what I try to convince myself each time I face another full flight of passengers," she said, wondering what he had in mind.

By the time they realized they were supposed to seat themselves, conversations had resumed. Diners once again busied themselves with plates heaped with food and energetically delivered it to their mouths.

At first glance, Trish had gathered that this was a

vegetable-free zone but a closer look told her that vegetables were available—as long as they were deep-fried. When she turned back to Larry, she interpreted his wink to mean he was on track and had already started his article.

They found a small table just as the older of the two waitresses hurried into the kitchen. The younger one stood talking with three burly men in work boots who were squeezed into a nearby booth. One thing was clear: People didn't *dine* here—here, food *fueled* people—people very different from the kind they saw in Manhattan.

After some minutes listening to teasing banter between the waitress and the men, Larry stood and walked over and, with exaggerated politeness, said to her, "Excuse me, but is there someone here who could wait on us?"

The waitress shrugged and looked back at the men. They smiled and folded their powerful, shirt-sleeved arms around their ample stomachs to listen.

"I'll see if I can find someone in a minute," she said, "just have a seat."

This would not have phased him in NY, but Larry stiffened, returned to Trish and tried to pull her to her feet.

Remembering an unruly passenger on one of her first flights, she resisted. "Larry, I'm *hungry.*"

Just then, the older waitress reappeared and stopped at their table. "What can I get you folks tonight?"

"Kind of hard to say without menus," Larry replied and sat down.

She shifted her weight like her feet hurt and said, "Well, we don't need them here. Most everybody who comes in always has the same thing—and knows what days we serve it."

"Tell us what's good tonight," Trish asked.

"That's catfish, fries, and hushpuppies, Sweetie. We don't serve alcohol, but any kind of iced tea you want."

"The owner's a *tea*-totaler," someone shouted, to general laughter.

Larry managed a smile and said, "From all the signs around for 'guns, and ammo,' he must be a hunter too."

"You got that right, mister," the waitress said. "He's out there right now. Hunting season opened yesterday, and most years he brings back mighty fine eating."

By the time they finished dinner and climbed in their car, crickets were chirping and shadows had filled the valley. Larry said, "I know that *New Yorker* readers will *love* this article." Trish was only half listening as Larry commented, with just the right touch of snark, about 'hefty sizes' and 'the hierarchy of appetites' while she sat and checked the directions the younger waitress had given her for places to overnight.

Several men passed their compact car with New York plates, and one in a plaid shirt poked his buddy, pointed at the back bumper, and gave Larry a smile and a two-fingered salute.

Unsure of the meaning, Larry muttered, "People who vote with their stomachs are unlikely to trust someone skinny like Obama."

"What about Jimmy Carter?" Trish said. "I think he was pretty trim." When she got no response, she said, "I think you should interview some of them."

He gave her a skeptical look and started the engine. The other vehicles in the lot now dwarfed their blue compact more conspicuously. "Come November, it'll be all uphill for any outsider down here," Larry blustered and pulled out onto the road.

With local radio to keep them awake, their headlights carved a path through the wooded hills as they curved and climbed. Their tired eyes had begun to blur, when a sign suddenly welcomed them to the town of McCracken, Georgia, "Home of the Chestnut Festival."

In response to the faded lettering, Larry said: "Good luck with that. I've read that those Chestnut trees are long gone—and the prospects for a comeback pretty shaky ... maybe someday, with new hybrids. And I can't believe that the grapes down here could have fared much better."

Sagging from fatigue, Trish said, "Well, we should find out more tomorrow."

She had never been around Larry this long at one stretch. Most of their time together had been at parties or public events where she felt more like an adornment or bystander than a participant while Larry dove into the fray to stir things up. He had a nose and an appetite for controversy. And he claimed the same for himself about wine.

The parking area of the lone motel in town was again crowded with trucks, all with rifle racks, and only one room was available. This time Larry hardly bothered to read any of the bumper stickers before they entered their room and saw that it had twin beds. After a day with so many jagged edges, Trish was relieved that Larry didn't complain about the sleeping arrangements.

She suspected he had other worries and felt a twinge of guilt. At the café, she had encouraged him to sample the local fare for the sake of authenticity while she ordered a fried egg, toast, and a glass of milk. Consequently, long after he turned in, she heard his bed complaining as he shifted to accommodate the hushpuppies and catfish roiling his stomach.

The next morning, Trish relished a simple motel breakfast

while Larry barely finished a cup of coffee. With directions provided by the desk clerk, they set out from McCracken to find their first Georgia winery.

Larry's mood failed to improve when the cell phone reception in the hills was spotty, and GPS instructions contradicted those of the motel clerk. After an hour and a half of guessing and back-tracking, the vineyards of Frogs Leap Winery abruptly appeared as they crested a hilltop.

"Why did you want to start with this winery?" Trish asked.

"Charlie Hanson lists it as one of the up-and-coming ones down here. But I don't think New York has anything to worry about. This way we make quick work of his opinion."

They pulled into the tasting room lot, sending up plumes of rust-colored dust, and waited for it to settle. To Larry's surprise, he noticed several other rental cars with New York plates. He got out and looped a thumb at one car with orange NY plates and said, "Let's get in there and see why they're here."

Trish gazed at the grape-clustered vines stretching along the contours and prepared to visit her first winery.

They entered and joined several other parties at the bar already in spirited conversation. While Larry eavesdropped, Trish picked up the tasting list and read as they waited for someone to serve them.

She started to ask Larry what to expect, but a finger to his lips told her he was listening to someone next to him. She caught a New York accent as Larry's neighbor told the couple next to him he'd come on the strength of Charlie Hanson's article in the *New Yorker*.

"How do you like the wine," Larry asked.

"We visited three wineries yesterday, and each got better. In fact, we feel lucky to taste at Frog's Leap today since it has become a wedding destination—that's the reason it's so hard to get any service."

Just then a harried waiter rushed in and said, "OK, who else wants to sample Leapfrog?" Ignoring Larry, he addressed Trish, "How about this attractive lady?"

Trish blushed and asked, "What do you recommend?"

While she listened to his suggestions, Larry leaned in closer and, sounding miffed, said, "We're together."

After their flights of whites and reds finally arrived, Larry gave each succeeding sample an ostentatious swirl and looked satisfied for the first time since they had met up at the airport.

When the couple next to them left, Larry asked his remaining neighbor, "Have you already been around to some of the other wineries here?"

"Yes," he answered and named two other vineyards.

"And you like this one best so far?"

"The owners know what they're doing. They moved here fifteen years ago from Upstate New York and bought this place. They've achieved amazing results with the soil around here."

"But the service here is still like in New York City," Larry said.

Trish wasn't sure, but he sounded like that was OKAY.

"Oh, you mean waiting, then being rushed? Anything worth going after is bound to be in demand."

"I've got to admit, it does make me feel at home," Larry said.

When their neighbor said goodbye and left, Larry turned to Trish. "As long as this place is best, we may as well stay a bit longer. No sense in wandering around. That should shorten our stay down here."

"But Larry, shouldn't you try a few other wineries to be above board?"

"I've seen enough of these hills, and I've got enough to get a letter printed as a follow-on to Charlie Hanson's article. We may just as well stay here for lunch."

By the time they left Frog's Leap, it was midafternoon and Trish was concerned about Larry taking the wheel. He had had what amounted to several glasses of wine working his way through the tasting list and then more with lunch.

Although she hadn't noticed any effect of alcohol on Larry at parties, neither of them had a car. Once, someone had challenged his opinion, and he withdrew to the edge of the fray, as though nursing some hurt from long ago. Her attempt to find out what was bothering him went nowhere, so she left it alone. Besides, staying out late didn't fit in with her need to rise early and get to the airport for her day's flight.

She fastened her seat belt and glanced at him as he pulled out on the road, and they took a different route from the way they had come.

"Now I'm ready to test the southern waters," he said. "I want to find out if my campaign stickers stir things up."

As they wound through the hills, he was having trouble handling the curves and Trish was about to mention it when she saw a sign for another vineyard. Larry slowed down, but noticing only a modest number of cars in the visitor's parking area, he sped up when Trish asked, "What about this one?"

"I think I already have everything I need," he said, without going into detail.

She wondered again why she had come along but left it at that. They had no definite plans about where to stay that night but had agreed to fly back to La Guardia the next evening; at least she was learning things about Larry that being about town with him had not shown her.

Before long they came up behind an older, slow-moving Lincoln plastered with bumper stickers and sporting a confederate flag. The car was surprisingly wide and moved at a tempo unimaginable for New Yorkers; the top of the driver's head barely showed above the dashboard, his arm stuck out the open window and plumes of cigar smoke trailed behind him.

"Now, here is a perfect specimen," Larry said with obvious relish. "I'll just get around him and see how he reacts to my blue state special."

However, since the road offered no possibility for passing, Larry got a sampling of local sentiments as they crept along and soaked up the messages of the Lincoln's bumper stickers in the billowing wake: *Global Warming? It's Called Summer, Stupid!* which soon got on his nerves.

At a point Larry judged wide enough to slip by—if the Lincoln eased over out of the center of the road—he honked and gestured to no avail and read: "*Anyone can honk, Tithe if you love Jesus,*" and began to cough.

Trish heard him mutter something about "cigars" and "like my father," and hoped he wouldn't do something rash.

Dark clouds had begun to gather by the time they reached the outskirts of a good-sized town. A reduced speed sign, posted at *Beatie's Fork Hardware and Hair Salon*, gave Larry hope of escaping from his trailing position. With a determined spurt, he passed his tormentor and slowed down directly in front of him.

"Take that, Cracker," he repeated with glee, keeping his eyes glued to the rear-view mirror. Despite Trish's scream, they rear-ended a dark pickup truck in the slowing traffic.

A second jolt came immediately as the Lincoln, now trailing behind, did the same to them and left their blue compact sandwiched between two vehicles caked with red Georgia clay.

The lone bumper sticker visible on the pickup ahead read: "*I'm in the NRA (and I'm not fond of tailgaters)*."

In surprisingly little time, the sheriff, lights flashing, arrived from his look-out where he had been waiting at the edge of town. He knocked on the window and asked, "Is anyone hurt?"

Larry lowered it and fumed, "Oh, for God's sake, I'm fine."

As the sheriff caught a whiff of Georgia wine alcohol, he raised his eyebrows and looked across at Trish. "And how about you, young lady? Are you alright?"

"Thank you. I'm fine, sir," she said, acutely aware it was a question Larry had not asked.

Turning back to Larry, the sheriff asked for his driver's license. "Well, well. New York. It looks like you were in too much of a hurry down here. And it smells like the lady should have been driving. You will have to come to the station so we can sort this out."

Hearing Larry blurt something about "snail-paced Georgia road hog," prompted Trish to straighten in her seat and say, "Larry, you don't have a clue." Surprising herself, she added, "I'm going home. I think you'll manage fine without an audience."

Larry seemed not to notice what she said, and the sheriff directed him to park at the curb and get into his cruiser.

At that, Trish got out of their blue car, collected her small rolling bag, and took out her phone. As the cruiser pulled away she tried to get a cab but had no cell phone reception. Unsure what to do, she continued into town.

Just as she reached a white, wooden frame house she stumbled and felt her left heel snag. It broke off and sent her reeling but she caught herself and looked around to size things up. A porch with several chairs on it stretched along the front of the house. Abandoned machinery and a car up on blocks filled the side yard; there was no sign of life.

Heavy rain began to fall and Trish limped across the yard to seek shelter on the porch. When the storm showed no signs of letting up, she knocked.

Eventually, an older man whose expression was hard to read, opened and asked, "Can I help you, young lady?"

"I am sorry to bother you, sir; I'm trying to get a taxi but there is no cell phone service. I need to get back to Atlanta and fly home tomorrow."

A woman's voice from inside called, "Who is it, Henry?"

Taking in Trish's bedraggled look, he said: "Edith, there's a young lady here who looks like she needs to warm up."

A woman his age in a blue apron and sensible shoes quickly appeared and said, "Well, with that storm out there, step aside Henry, and invite her in."

"Oh, thank you," Trish said, "You are just like my grandmother back in Kansas."

Before she knew it, Trish was seated in the Stubbins's kitchen with a steaming cup of tea and telling her story. As it turned out, Henry was an old friend of the sheriff and promised to see what could be done for 'her friend from New York'. Meanwhile, they insisted that Trish have supper with them and stay the night. She could catch the bus to Atlanta in the morning.

After supper, Trish heard Henry talking on the phone with the sheriff, and a knock came on her door.

"Well, it looks as if your friend will be nice and dry tonight— he'll spend it in jail. Most likely be released on bail tomorrow. Let us know if you need anything."

"Oh, thank you, for everything," she said and immediately felt better.

That night, however, she couldn't sleep. Was she treating Larry unfairly? Nobody is perfect. But was there no room in his calculations for other people's feelings? Had New York changed him?

She decided there would still be time to change her mind in the morning about leaving and finally fell asleep.

After Mrs. Stubbins fed her enough breakfast 'to travel on,' Henry drove Trish to the bus stop in his aging Buick. When they pulled up across from the courthouse on the town square, it was hard for her to leave the cocoon of warmth so familiar to her from back in Kansas. She again thanked Henry and promised to let them know as soon as she arrived safely back in New York but caught herself wondering: Would Larry be going out in one of those chain gangs in orange suits she had seen collecting trash along the road yesterday?

Then she realized that whether he deserved it or not wasn't up to her, and she felt calm for the first time since leaving New York. What was up to her was when and where to take another bite out of the Big Apple.

Ashes To Asheville

On the evening of August 26th, in the Piedmont region of North Carolina, five-year old Addie Beaux sat on her father's lap as chill mountain air crept down the slopes to the town of Valdese and mingled with the shroud of grainy wood smoke hanging above their small house. Snuggling into his secure embrace near the crackling fire, Addie eagerly awaited the story she first had heard before she learned to talk.

Her father's words came to her before he spoke them, and they both knew he could rely on her to correct him if his memory faltered. As he rocked her, she begged to hear it from him again before she drifted off:

"On a Friday in August of 1689, our Waldensian ancestors huddled in the woods and villages near Geneva, Switzerland. They were waiting for the streets to darken under the somber clouds above the big lake. Evening church bells finally rang and small groups of men—some of them with guns—stole away to the lakeshore and climbed into boats. Fog muffled the sound of their oars, and they crossed from Switzerland on their way back to Savoy."

At this point in the story, Addie would ask, "Weren't they afraid, Bo?"

"I suppose they were, Addie, but they had been away a long time," he allowed "but now they were going home. Our ancestors had been forced to leave the steep valleys of Italy's Piedmont and take refuge in Switzerland. Every year in August, we celebrate that journey over the Alps into Savoy and call it 'the Glorious Return'."

"Why did they have to leave, Bo?"

He slowed, and then stopped rocking. "To be free, Addie. Sometimes you have to make sacrifices to live the way you believe is right. Waldensians left Savoy so they could worship the way they want. And they stayed away until that night in August when it was safe to return."

She imagined figures huddled in a boat and shivered when it drifted into a fog bank. Bo held her close and resumed rocking until she again relaxed. Twisting around on his lap and bracing against her father's chest, she asked, "Is that where Mommy went too?"

"No, Sweetheart. The Glorious Return was a long time ago. Mommy got sick three years after you were born ... she had to go to heaven to get better."

"Did she go in a boat?"

"No, she's buried right here in Valdese. The Waldensians went in boats though. And your Gran's parents came here in a boat. They left that Piedmont a hundred years ago and came right here to our Piedmont in North Carolina where it's safe to practice our faith."

Addie settled back down. "Did Gran ever go back," she yawned?

"No. Gran talked about visiting there once, but we miss

CHAPTER 2

WHY CAN'T I SEE?

SAMSON

THE STORY

"I stand here with my hands on the pillars, blinded, but the truth is I was blind long before I lost my sight. Every compromise and every reckless decision led me deeper into this trap. I didn't see how enthralled I'd become until it was too late. Delilah's intentions were never hidden, yet I chose not to see. But now... now I feel it. The strength I wasted—rising in me once more. Thank you, God, for the chance to please You. The pillars shift beneath my hands. The weight groans above me, and with one final breath... I push.

THE STUDY

Scripture: *Galatians 5:16 (ESV) - "But I say, walk by the Spirit, and you will not gratify the desires of the flesh."*

Samson was a man, chosen by God to be a judge and given supernatural strength. Yet, he wasn't walking in the Spirit—he was led by impulse, attraction, and unchecked desire. His downfall was ignoring the signs of obvious betrayal and playing games with his anointing. Each time Delilah pressed him for the secret of his strength, he inched closer to revealing it, playing with the very thing that would destroy him. Ultimately, he lost more than his power; he lost his sight, freedom, and nearly his destiny.

Like Samson, we can fall into the trap of loving the very thing that is out to kill us. The world is filled with Delilah's temptations, which draw us into a false sense of safety while stripping away our strength. Whether it's relationships, habits, or desires that lead us away from God, the pattern remains the same: we hold on too long, ignore the warning signs, and wake up too late… if we wake up at all.

The Seduction of Sin

Samson didn't set out to throw away the calling God placed on his life, but he lost sight of God's will and blindly chased his own. He believed he was in complete control of his life. This is how sin works: It often appears in subtle choices that quietly chip away at our faith, rather than a bold act of rebellion. We convince ourselves, "Just this once," "It's not that bad," or "I can handle it." But like Samson, we fail to see that each compromise weakens us, making the next one easier. The enemy is patient. He doesn't mind if it takes time. Like Delilah, he presses persistently, knowing that if we stay in the wrong place long enough, we will eventually give in.

How Sin Whispers,
"Just Stay a Little Longer…"

Samson had every opportunity to walk away, but he didn't. The warnings were clear; each time Delilah tried to bind him, he should have known she meant him harm. Yet, he stayed. He convinced himself that he was still strong enough to handle it.

How often do we do the same? We recognize the warning signs: a habit forming, a conviction softening, a standard shifting. Yet we stay because it feels good, seems harmless, and we believe we can manage it. And just like Samson, we don't realize how far we've fallen until we've lost what made us strong.

Breaking Free Before You Lose Everything

God has called us to be set apart, to walk in His strength, and to recognize the dangers of compromise before they take root. *Romans 6:12* reminds us, *"Let not sin therefore reign in your mortal body, that ye should obey it in the lusts thereof."* Strength is not found in testing our limits but in knowing when to walk away.

Take a Moment to Reflect: Pg. 89

- What is keeping you spiritually blind—what are you refusing to see clearly?
- Have you allowed repeated compromise to weaken your spiritual strength?
- Who or what in your life feels safe but is actually a trap?
- What would change if you truly walked by the Spirit instead of your impulses?

Maybe the real danger isn't what you're holding on to—it's what you've stopped fighting for. Strength doesn't come from white-knuckling sin; it comes from recognizing what's been slowly draining you. What if the blindness isn't just from compromise, but from refusing to let go of what you think you need? Ask God to help you see what you've ignored and to give you the courage to confront it.

Call to Action:

Break up with the thing that's blinding you. Call it out. Cut it off. You know what's been weakening your walk—now do something about it. Walk in the calling God has given you. Open your eyes and be strong!

Samson's downfall was personal, but the enemy's strategy goes beyond individuals. He doesn't just deceive people; he infiltrates families, communities, and churches. His most dangerous work is done secretly through gradual shifts that go unnoticed. What happens when deception becomes so familiar that we mistake it for truth?

CHAPTER 3

CAN I HAVE BOTH?

JEZEBEL

THE STORY

"They call me the Villain, the Seductress, the Destroyer of Prophets. Please—such outdated labels. I prefer Influencer, Reformer, and Liberator. You may think it's hard to pull people away from their God. It's not. You don't rip the truth out of their hands, you dilute it; a whisper here, a question there. "Did God really say?" That has always been the starting point of every compromise. I didn't come with harsh commands—I came with tolerance. With softness. With words that sound like freedom: inclusion, compassion, equity. I taught them that truth is subjective. That holiness is harmful. That conviction is violence. And they ate it up like honey on the altar. I didn't need to force them to bow to Baal. I just gave them permission to blend. Keep your worship—just tweak the lyrics. Keep your God—just redefine Him. A small compromise, a hint of comfort, and soon they couldn't distinguish between the sacred and the sensual.

The prophets of God stood in my way, of course—bold men with fire in their mouths. So, I silenced them. Not with swords— oh no, that's too messy. I utilized shame, called them intolerant and dangerous, and I made them afraid to speak. And those who didn't bow? I buried them beneath my empire of charm. Now look at them. Spinning in circles, quoting fragments of scripture they no longer believe in. Worshipping a God they've remodeled in their own image. They can continue to think they're serving God, completely unaware that their fire has gone out. And me? I'm still here. Painting compromises in glitter, dressing deception in love. Because if I can't make you curse your God, I'll make you blend Him with everything He hates."

THE STUDY

Scripture: *Revelation 18:4-5 (ESV) - "Come out of her, my people, lest you take part in her sins, lest you share in her plagues; for her sins are heaped high as heaven..."*

The voice of Jezebel didn't end with Ahab's court—it echoes through time, disguised as modern virtue. She seduces not just individuals, but entire cultures and systems. Revelation calls her Babylon, but her strategy hasn't changed: seduce, mix, distort, and destroy. The warning remains: Come out from her. Don't partner with the compromise she offers. Don't drink what she's serving just because it's popular. If you do, you won't just lose truth, you'll share in her judgment.

Jezebel was not an enemy who attacked with open warfare. She was far more dangerous than that. She was a master manipulator, one who knew that the best way to destroy the people of God was not to oppose them directly, but to make them feel at ease with making certain allowances. She did not demand that Israel abandon God entirely; she simply convinced them to include other gods alongside Him. Little by little, she led them into spiritual corruption, cloaking her agenda in the language of tolerance and inclusion.

Her methods don't always ask believers to reject God; she suggests that they mix faith with the world, watering down convictions in the name of unity. Jezebel understood something crucial: outright destruction is not as effective as slow deception. If people willingly allow compromises, they will eventually turn away from God altogether.

Distracting You is the Best way to Destroy You

Jezebel knew she could distract God's people by introducing new gods, subtly shifting the people's focus. She claimed it would be more progressive, inclusive, and open-minded. Over time, what was once unthinkable became normalized. The same strategy is evident today. Culture pressures believers to "update" their beliefs, modernizing doctrine to align with contemporary values. The world pushes the idea that exclusivity in faith is intolerance, that holding firm to biblical truth is outdated. Just as Israel was lured into compromise under Jezebel's rule, many believers today are tempted to soften their faith for the sake of fitting in.

Using Culture to Pull the Church Away

The spirit of Jezebel seeks to erode truth by mixing it with falsehood. It convinces people that standing firm on God's Word is unkind, that holding to absolute truth is offensive. It silences prophets and preachers who refuse to conform, just as Jezebel killed the prophets who spoke against her agenda *(1 Kings 18:4)*. The goal is always the same: to reshape faith so that it becomes indistinguishable from the surrounding culture.

How does this manifest in our lives? It can be subtle, lowering our standards, compromising moral convictions, or justifying things that we once knew were wrong. It can be in churches that shift their teaching to avoid offending or in believers who begin to tolerate what they once rejected. The issue is not the presence of compromise but our ability to recognize it.

Recognize and Resist the Enemy's Traps

Elijah stood against Jezebel, refusing to be silenced. When the prophets of Baal were defeated, Jezebel sought to intimidate him into retreat. The enemy still uses intimidation today—fear of rejection, fear of being labeled judgmental, fear of standing alone. But just as Elijah remained faithful, we must stand firm in a world that pressures us to conform.

Revelation 2:20 warns against tolerating Jezebel: *"Nevertheless, I have this against you: You tolerate that woman Jezebel, who calls herself a prophetess and teaches and deceives my servants to commit sexual immorality and to eat meat sacrificed to idols."* The charge is not just against Jezebel herself but against those who tolerate her influence.

Take a Moment to Reflect: Pg. 91

- Where have you allowed modern culture to shape your understanding of God's truth?
- Are you mixing faith with popular opinions to avoid offense?
- Have you redefined sin as 'progress,' or truth as 'judgmental'?
- What parts of your belief system need to be realigned with the word of God?

Not everything that sounds kind is rooted in truth. Sometimes, what we label as compassion is just fear of confrontation. Sometimes, what we call tolerance is just spiritual fatigue. If your convictions feel quieter lately, if truth feels blurrier, it's worth asking—what voices have you been listening to? And more importantly, when did God's voice stop being the loudest?

Call to Action:

You have to choose—there's no middle ground. Truth doesn't blend, and faith doesn't bow. Make your decision, and make it loud and clear. Don't entertain what God has condemned. Don't stay silent when deception starts speaking. Plant

CHAPTER 1: **HOW DID I GET HERE?**

What small decisions led you closer to something you once knew was dangerous?

_____
_____
_____
_____
_____
_____
_____
_____

Have you settled near something God warned you to stay far from?

_____
_____
_____
_____
_____
_____
_____
_____

In what ways has your spiritual environment changed without you realizing it?

_____
_____
_____
_____
_____
_____
_____
_____

Are you mistaking comfort for peace—and ignoring the warning signs?

_____
_____
_____
_____
_____
_____
_____
_____

CHAPTER 2: **WHY CAN'T I SEE?**

What is keeping you spiritually blind—what are you refusing to see clearly?

_____

_____

_____

_____

_____

_____

_____

_____

Have you allowed repeated compromise to weaken your spiritual strength?

_____

_____

_____

_____

_____

_____

_____

_____

Who or what in your life feels safe but is actually a trap?

_____
_____
_____
_____
_____
_____
_____
_____
_____

What would change if you truly walked by the Spirit instead of your impulses?

_____
_____
_____
_____
_____
_____
_____
_____
_____

CHAPTER 3: **CAN I HAVE BOTH?**

Where have you allowed modern culture to shape your understanding of God's truth?

_____
_____
_____
_____
_____
_____
_____
_____

Are you blending faith with popular opinions to avoid offense?

_____
_____
_____
_____
_____
_____
_____
_____

Have you redefined sin as 'progress,' or truth as 'judgmental'?

_____

_____

_____

_____

_____

_____

_____

_____

What parts of your belief system need to be realigned with the word of God?

_____

_____

_____

_____

_____

_____

_____

_____

CHAPTER 4: **WHAT AM I FORGETTING?**

What distractions are keeping you from spending intentional
time with God?

_____
_____
_____
_____
_____
_____
_____
_____

Have you replaced rest with productivity, and connection with
busyness?

_____
_____
_____
_____
_____
_____
_____
_____

When was the last time you truly paused just to be with God?

_____
_____
_____
_____
_____
_____
_____
_____

What do you need to remove from your life to make room for real spiritual renewal?

_____
_____
_____
_____
_____
_____
_____
_____

CHAPTER 5: CAN I RESIST?

When did your spiritual urgency begin to fade—and what replaced it?

_____
_____
_____
_____
_____
_____
_____
_____

How do you discern between comfort and compromise in your daily choices?

_____
_____
_____
_____
_____
_____
_____
_____

What lies have you accepted that once would've shocked you?

_____
_____
_____
_____
_____
_____
_____
_____

If Satan were to slowly disarm your faith, what tactic would he likely use, and has he already started?

_____
_____
_____
_____
_____
_____
_____
_____

CHAPTER 6: **IS IT THAT BAD?**

What part of your past are you still defending, even though God called you out of it?

_____
_____
_____
_____
_____
_____
_____
_____

Is there something you've romanticized that is enslaving you?

_____
_____
_____
_____
_____
_____
_____
_____

Are you holding onto sentimentality, and is it keeping you from obedience?

_____
_____
_____
_____
_____
_____
_____
_____

What would complete surrender look like if you stopped trying to hold on to God and the world?

_____
_____
_____
_____
_____
_____
_____
_____

CHAPTER 7: HOW MUCH MORE?

What have you convinced yourself God would never ask you to give up?

_____
_____
_____
_____
_____
_____
_____
_____

Are you clinging to something good that's quietly keeping you from something greater?

_____
_____
_____
_____
_____
_____
_____
_____

Is your obedience shaped more by convenience or by conviction?

_____

_____

_____

_____

_____

_____

_____

_____

If Jesus walked away today, what would you still be standing next to?

_____

_____

_____

_____

_____

_____

_____

_____

CHAPTER 8: **WHO DO I BELIEVE?**

Do I recognize the difference between a comforting voice and a truthful one?

_____
_____
_____
_____
_____
_____
_____
_____

Have I put more faith in a personality than in the presence of God?

_____
_____
_____
_____
_____
_____
_____
_____

How do I test the voices and teachings I allow to shape my beliefs?

_____

_____

_____

_____

_____

_____

_____

_____

When was the last time I questioned whether something 'Christian' was actually biblical?

_____

_____

_____

_____

_____

_____

_____

_____

CHAPTER 9: **WHAT ABOUT EVERYONE ELSE?**

Have I already decided what I'll do when no one else is standing?

_____
_____
_____
_____
_____
_____
_____
_____

What pressures have I quietly surrendered to in the name of peace?

_____
_____
_____
_____
_____
_____
_____
_____

Am I living in a way that reminds the world who I belong to?

_____

_____

_____

_____

_____

_____

_____

_____

What would it cost me to stand—and am I willing to pay that price?

_____

_____

_____

_____

_____

_____

_____

_____

CHAPTER 10: WHY AM I SO SLEEPY?

Have I mistaken spiritual activity for true intimacy with God?

_____
_____
_____
_____
_____
_____
_____
_____

What have I left 'in process' that God already told me to finish?

_____
_____
_____
_____
_____
_____
_____
_____

What warning signs have I been ignoring because I still feel comfortable?

_____
_____
_____
_____
_____
_____
_____
_____

If I keep living at this pace, where will I be one year from now—closer to God or further away?

_____
_____
_____
_____
_____
_____
_____
_____